BERRIES IN THE SCOOP

ROUNDABOUT AMERICA

Come, let us look at the ways of life
in our country. Let us go into out-of-the-way
corners, up on the hills and down in the
valleys, into city streets and village homes.
Let us see and get to know the people.
Here and there, round about America, are
friends worth knowing.

The *Roundabout America* stories
are vivid scenes from real life,
in short-story or longer form,
for younger readers.

BERRIES
in the SCOOP
A CAPE COD CRANBERRY
STORY *by* LOIS LENSKI

J. B. LIPPINCOTT COMPANY · PHILADELPHIA & NEW YORK

Foreword

Come with me to Cape Cod on a mellow autumn day. We will follow a quiet country road with the blue sea on one side and purple cranberry bogs on the other. Some bogs are peaceful and undisturbed, with crows and wild ducks flying overhead. Others are noisy with trucks that come and go, and people hard at work. Brown-skinned Portuguese children laugh and shout, fall into ditches and jump out again, play games and never tire. The sun is warm upon my back, as I borrow a scoop, drop on my knees and gather cranberries to fill my box.

Who, in America, has not enjoyed the tart taste of the cranberry with his turkey at Thanksgiving? They were growing wild in the marshes of Cape Cod when the Pilgrims landed. The Indians mixed them with wild deer meat for pemmican. The colonists sent a barrel of them back home to King Charles II. In the more than two centuries since then, they have become an American institution.

The word "bog" is misleading. Actually a cranberry bog in the growing and picking season is dry, though the roots below the sand are deep in peat soil that comes from *the marshes. Ditches cross the bogs to drain off the water and help in flooding. Higher dikes serve as truck roads. The bogs are small, intimate and beautiful, rimmed around with pines.*

My thanks to the Oak Grove School children at Onset, Massachusetts, who gave me this story.

Lois Lenski

Contents

Verses

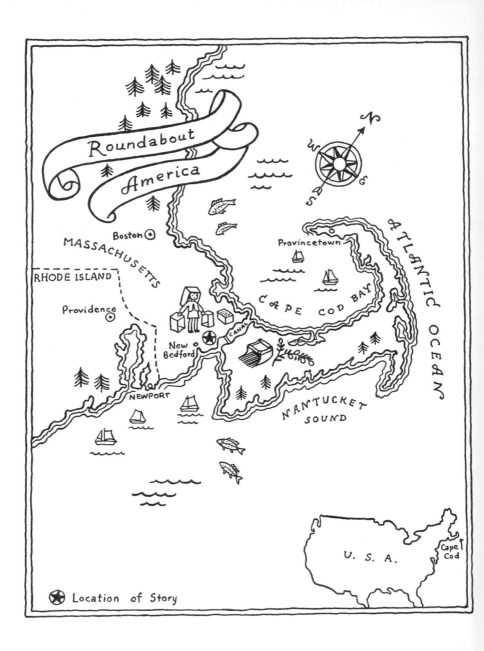

Going to the Bog

You have to wear warm clothing,
　　It's windy in the truck;
You'd better put a hat on,
　　Or you may get sun struck!

You must wear shoes and lace them,
　　Put rubbers on, you bet!
Because of all the floodings,
　　The bog is sort of wet!

You have to take your dinner,
　　A sandwich thick or pie;
You're apt to get so hungry,
　　You think that you will die!

Your back gets tired of bending
　　To scoop up berries red,
But when the day is over
　　You can go home to bed!

CHAPTER ONE

Kayla at Home

"Old lady witch
Fell in the ditch;
She found a penny
And thought she was rich.

Old lady witch,
You let me be!
I'll run off
Before you catch me!"

The little girls sang the words. Then they ran up to the witch, teasing her. She chased them, but they ran back to the fence.

Kayla Santos was the witch. They were playing in front of her house. Along the narrow road were other small houses with fences. The road was called Aunt Hannah's Lane. Perhaps a hundred years before, a kind Aunt Hannah had lived there. Now she and her old home were gone. Only her name remained.

Kayla thought the road was named for her own Aunt Tana. No one had told her different. Aunt Tana lived with Uncle Diamond in the house down at the corner by the store of Peter Dias.

The little girls took turns playing witch. They shouted and laughed as they ran.

It was August. The sun shone hot and bright upon Cape Cod. The sky was blue with white clouds. The air was clear and clean. It smelled of the ocean not far away.

"Look, there comes Lukie Lima!" cried Sistie Mendes.

A boy came riding by on a bicycle. Other boys came running, trying to keep up. Julio and Roberto, Kayla's brothers, came out.

"Lukie can ride without using his hands or the pedals!" said Joey Mendes.

"Sometime he might fall," said Timmy, Lukie's brother.

"Let's see you do it, Lukie," said Julio. "Ride down Aunt Tana's Lane to the cranberry bog."

Lukie stood still and did not go. He was a good boy with a happy smile on his face. His black hair was curly. The boys teased him about it.

"Look at his curls!" said Roberto. "Do you take your mother's curls off at night, Lukie?"

Lukie reached over, but Roberto ducked.

Lukie stood by his bicycle and did not go.

"Well, let *me* try it, Lukie," said Nicky Lopez. "Give me your bike."

Lukie said, "No, you'll wreck it."

"*Can* you do it, Lukie?" asked Kayla. "Ride without using your hands and feet?"

"I don't believe it," said Isabel Lopez, called Izzie for short.

"You gotta show me!" said Josie, her sister.

Lukie looked at Kayla.

"I'll show *you*," he said.

Off he went, arms high in the air and legs outspread. The bicycle bumped over the ruts. He went sailing down the hill.

The children shouted: *"Lukie likes Kayla! Lukie likes Kayla!"*

Kayla was ashamed. She ran to her gate. She started to go in the house.

Down the road, Lukie turned off into the cranberry bog. The children waited until he came back. Kayla waited too. Lukie had to pedal hard up the hill.

He held a bunch of cranberries in his hand.

"They're still green," said Nicky Lopez. "They're no good."

"They won't get red until fall," said his sister Josie. "Any dumb kid ought to know that."

"Gee! I can hardly wait till picking time," said Sistie Mendes. "It's fun to scoop."

"I go to the bog all the time with my Aunt Tana," said Kayla. "My Aunt Tana is the fastest scooper around here!"

"Who told you that?"

Isabel Lopez came up and faced her. Josie came, too.

"Our mother can scoop faster than your old Aunt Tana!" said Izzie. *"Our mother's* the fastest scooper in this town!"

Kayla closed her lips and said nothing. It was sometimes hard to be friends with the Lopez girls.

"Oh, you keep still, you girls!" said Lukie Lima. "My grandmother's the best! One day she scooped 119 boxes!"

"Golly! Whoever heard of that?" laughed Julio. "Did she scoop all day and all night?"

Izzie Lopez put her hands on her hips. She looked straight at Kayla.

"Nobody *ever* scooped 100 boxes in a day!"

she said. She turned to Lukie. "You better stop telling lies . . ."

Lukie got on his bike and rode off. "Who's going to the store?" he cried. The boys followed.

Kayla stood by her gate as the girls walked away.

"Kayla! Kayla!"

She heard her mother calling. She ran in the house.

The house was not very large. It had three small rooms downstairs, the living room, the kitchen and Grandma's bedroom. Kayla slept on a cot in the room with her grandmother. Upstairs were two low bedrooms, one for her parents and one for the boys.

Grandma and Mother were sewing. The sewing machine was noisy. It needed oiling. It was hard to hear what Mother was saying. She was talking to Grandma in a low voice.

Kayla waited till she stopped the machine. Mother was making her a bathing suit. She had wanted a new red one and had picked it out at the store in Onset. But there was no money to buy it. So Mother had ripped up an old dress of her own. She had cut out a bathing suit for Kayla. She was sewing it now. But it was not pretty. It was brown and Kayla did not like it.

"Go and feed the chickens," said Mother. "And bring in a head of cabbage from the garden."

She turned to the old lady. "Good thing we got cabbage to eat."

"There's plenty corn, too," said Grandma. "It will soon be ready to pick."

Grandma and Mother spoke in Portuguese when they talked together. They spoke English to the children.

When Kayla came back, Mother said, "Light the oil stove. Put on a kettle of water to heat, Kayla."

The women went on talking. Kayla worked quietly so she could listen. She understood Portuguese, though she only spoke it when she had to.

"Frank says he's going to be laid off again." said Mother. "Then there will be no money at all."

Kayla's father worked at a factory in New Bedford. He came home each week end, riding in another worker's car.

"We need money," said Mother. "They would bring a good price, if you'd sell them."

Grandma shook her head. Her worn face was wrinkled and brown. Her eyes were sad.

"Why can't you sell just one piece?" asked Mother. "You never wear it anyhow. What good does it do you?"

Again Grandma shook her head. Kayla saw that her worn old hands trembled. The old lady could hardly hold her needle.

"Never," said Grandma. "It is for one of my granddaughters."

Mother laughed. "If you give it to the daughter of any one of my sisters, you know what they will do? Run to the nearest jewelry store. They will sell it all quick for money, money! It's money they want!"

"It must never be sold," said Grandma. "It must be handed down from one generation to the next. It must be kept in the family—always."

Mother looked up and saw Kayla standing by the door. She changed her tone.

"Our money always runs out by summertime," she said. "And our food supplies at the same time. They never last till the next cranberry season."

"There's always a way," said Grandma. "God will help us."

"It will be weeks before the cranberries are ripe," said Mother.

"We can wait," said Grandma. "We have cabbage and potatoes, corn and squash in the garden. We can kill off the hens . . ."

"Not while they are laying," said Mother. "We need the eggs."

"Don't forget the quahogs," said Grandma. "We can go to the beach and dig them. God put the quahogs in the ocean for us. We do not need to go hungry."

Quahogs are hard-shell clams. Kayla had

often seen her father dry-dig them on Back
Beach. She had seen men raking them up with
basket rakes. Sometimes they went out in boats
and used tongs on the hard bottom of the ocean.

"Quahogs!" laughed Mother. "Yes! Un-
less the *bravas* have got the shores all dug up,
and there is nothing left!"

Portuguese people are known as *bravas* on
Cape Cod.

The large quahogs made good chowder.
Kayla liked to eat it for supper, cooked with
potatoes and onions. The small steamed qua-

hogs were good, too. She never tired of them.

Mother went out in the kitchen.

"Come, Kayla," said Grandma.

They went into Grandma's tiny bedroom. They sat on Kayla's cot. Grandma opened the round-topped trunk under her bed. She brought out a small box. It was made of olive wood.

"I brought this from the old country," she said.

"From the Isle of Vincent in the Azores," repeated Kayla, who had learned it by heart.

She had found the spot on a map at school. It was a tiny speck in the great Atlantic Ocean, off the shore of Portugal. Grandma had told her about it.

"And Grandpa came from Cape Verde," Kayla added. "He was a blacksmith. He used to shoe horses before he died."

"When I first came here," said Grandma, "I was young and had to work hard. I did housework in Fall River. Grandpa worked in the textile mills. We sent for our children one at a time. We built a home. We sent our children to school. They learned English. All my children learned to read."

Grandma opened the box on her lap. She took out some pieces of jewelry. There were a gold bracelet and a pair of gold earrings. There was a pretty brooch set with pearls. Grandma picked them up one by one. She held them in her hands.

"These are heirlooms," said Grandma. *"My grandma gave them to me when I married. I was the oldest granddaughter. They are solid gold and very valuable. I am keeping them for my granddaughters. I brought them from the old country. They must never be sold."*

Kayla touched the pearl brooch. It was very pretty.

"You like it?" Grandma pinned it on the

front of Kayla's dress. Grandma and Kayla were close friends. Kayla gave Grandma a kiss.

"Now I will put it back in the box," said Grandma.

Kayla hated to take Grandma's gold pin off. "Can I wear it sometime?" she asked.

Grandma smiled. "When the right time comes," she said. "When you get married—yes! It will be a present on your wedding day!"

"Oh, but that's too long to wait!" said Kayla. "I mean *now*."

She would like to show it to her girl friends. What would the Lopez girls say if they saw it?

Grandma shook her head.

"Never forget this, Kayla," she said. "These things *must never be sold. They must stay in the family.*"

Kayla nodded. "I will remember, Grandma," she said. "I will not forget."

After supper Kayla went to bed early, but

not to sleep. She kept thinking about the pretty bracelet, the earrings and the gold pin.

She watched Grandma get ready for bed. She saw her kneel and say her prayers. She saw her open her trunk and put the olive-wood box away. She saw her lock the trunk. And she watched where she put the key.

At last Kayla fell asleep.

CHAPTER TWO

Kayla's Picnic

"I like to go on a picnic," said Kayla.

"We'll catch a lot of little fishes," said Roberto.

Kayla carried a gallon bottle in her hand. Her brother dragged empty potato bags behind him.

It was Sunday morning. The family had all been to church. Now the children walked through the pine woods. The pine needles felt soft to their bare feet. They wore bathing suits, for the August day was hot. Kayla wore the brown one that Mother had made. Beyond the pine woods lay the blue sea and the white sandy beach.

The day before, Mother had said, "There is no money to buy meat."

Grandma had answered, "We will go and dig quahogs."

Kayla had clapped her hands. "Let's have a picnic!"

Father had come home from New Bedford. He had been laid off, just as he said. Uncle Tony had come from Taunton in his car to spend Saturday night. Mother had asked the aunts and uncles and cousins to come along on the picnic. Everybody in the family enjoyed a picnic on the beach in the summertime.

The children walked. The old people rode in Uncle Tony's car.

"First we eat dinner!" said Father when they got to the beach.

"Bring out the picnic baskets!" said Uncle Diamond.

"I'm hungry," said Julio. "I want some *jag* to eat."

Some of the people sat on the dry sand. Kayla helped Aunt Minietta spread out blankets. Cousins Nancy and Ruby helped too. The men brought a car seat from Uncle Tony's car. Kayla helped set out the food.

Aunt Donna and Aunt Tana both brought large pots of *d'jagaseda,* called *jag* for short. It was lima beans cooked with onions and rice. It had *linguisa*–spicy frankfurters on top.

Besides the pots of *jag,* there were fried green bananas, pickles, corn-meal rolls and other good things to eat. Everybody drank soda out of paper cups. They ate watermelon to top it all off.

Little Bubba, Aunt Donna's boy, got up from his mother's lap. He threw sand on the food and on people's heads.

At first they laughed. Then Aunt Tana jumped up and spanked him.

"You let him alone!" cried Aunt Donna. "He's *my* boy."

"Why don't *you* spank him then?" asked Aunt Tana.

The women gathered up the dishes.

"Before you kids run off to swim," said Uncle Tony, "come and help dig quahogs."

The boys and men hung potato bags on their belts. They walked in the water with bare feet. Kayla went with them. The cousins, Marcella and Ruby and Nancy went too. They all had bags except Kayla.

"You can put your quahogs in my bag," said Nancy.

"But how do you find a quahog?" asked Kayla.

"I'll show you," said Nancy. "You feel it in the sand with your toes. If it's something *round,* it's a quahog. If it's something *pointy,* it's a snail. We don't eat snails."

Kayla laughed. The men and boys picked quahogs up and put them in their bags.

Each quahog is like a clam. It has two shells fastened together. The meat is inside. It has to be split open to get the meat out. The meat is good to eat.

Kayla tried and tried, but she could not find any. Once or twice she picked up stones. Nancy laughed at her. Nancy's bag was getting heavy. She kept on looking for more.

Kayla saw Roberto digging holes in the sand. She ran over and stood beside him. Catching little fishes was more fun than digging quahogs.

"Did you save the paper cups?" asked Kayla.

"Yes," said Roberto. He had a pile of them.

Kayla dug little holes in the sand, too. The tide came in and washed over them.

"The fishes will think our holes are good places to hide," said Kayla.

"There's a fish!" cried Roberto.

The tide had rolled out. Roberto was very quick. He put a paper cup down on top of the hole. He picked the fish up in the cup. He put his hand over it. Then he dumped it into the glass bottle.

Kayla laughed. She found more little fishes. Cousin Nancy left her quahogs and came over—

"Mine are goldfish," said Kayla. "I wish I could get some goldfish food for them."

Nancy said, "They are silver, not gold."

Kayla said, "I don't care. I will take them home. Oh, I hope they won't die . . ."

Father came back, his bag heavy with qua-hogs. He dug a large hole in the sand. Roberto put rocks in the hole. Father had matches and they built a fire of sticks on the rocks. Kayla and Nancy brought water in a can from the ocean.

Julio went to the woods. He brought some smooth sticks. The men came back with their bags. The women came over and they all put quahogs on the sticks. They held them over the fire. The shells opened up.

Some quahogs they ate raw. Some they took out and fried. Some they steamed over the can of water. Everybody ate quahogs and said they were good. There were still plenty to take home, to eat through the week.

The children played hide-and-seek in the woods near the beach. The boys played ball in the water. They threw a rubber ball in the water and swam after it. Whoever got the ball threw it in again. They all tried to catch it.

The boys were very much at home in the ocean. They swam like fish. They dived down and came up. They knew no fear of the water.

"Let's play *Swordfish!*" cried Cousin Don.

He had found a large board floating in the water. Each boy had a small stick for a play knife.

"This board's a swordfish," said Don. "Here it comes after you."

Roberto tried to hit it, but the swordfish got away. Roberto swam under water. He brought up a large rock.

"We've got the gold," he said.

At the magic word, the other boys turned into pirates. They swam after Roberto and stole his gold. Then he chased the pirates, but they all got away from him.

Julio, still in the water, put the board on his back. He tied it there with a rope. Little Bubba ran out in the water to see what he was doing. Julio picked the boy up. He put him on his back on top of the board.

"I'm a horse and Bubba's a cowboy!" shouted Julio. "The board is my saddle. Watch us go!"

Julio dived under, pushing ahead in the water. Bubba kept hitting him with a stick.

He cried, "Yippy, Yippy! I'm a cowboy!"

Bubba was heavy to carry. So Julio ran to shore and dumped him off.

Now the aunts came wading in the water. Marcella and Ruby came too. Aunt Pell was the most fun. She liked to play with the children. She waded out waist-deep.

Suddenly she tripped and fell over. An under-water swimmer had taken her by both feet and tripped her. She could not see who it was.

"Oh, a crab bit me!" she cried. She ran back to the beach.

Horseflies flew around her head and stung her. They stung like bumblebees. She ran into the water again.

"I'll get that crab and break his shell!" she cried. She chased the children into the water.

"Hey! One of you kids tripped me. Who was it?" she called. "Hey, you little crows, who was it?"

But no one told her. They all swam away.

Roberto found a dead jellyfish. He came

back and threw it. It landed on Aunt Pell's back.

"What's on my back?" she cried. "What's on me?"

Kayla ran out to her and took the jellyfish off. Nancy and Ruby ran in the water again.

Kayla and Aunt Pell ran up to the dry sand. They were out of breath. They sat down by the aunts and uncles. The old people were talking about cranberries. They were always talking about cranberries and making money.

"Cranberry money is not so bad," said Uncle Tony. "You work hard for six weeks or two months. Then you can loaf for the rest of the year."

"If there are three or four people picking," said Father, "they can make a couple thousand. But they got to be good."

"We have to pay our taxes with cranberry money," said Mother. "We have to buy oil for fuel and our winter food supplies. We have to pay our debts. And we ought to save a little."

"Julio can scoop this year," said Father. "He's big and strong for twelve."

"But he should stay in school," said Mother.

"I kept all my children in school," said Grandma. "They all learned to read."

"Julio wants to quit school and work," said Mother.

"I've been picking cranberries for fifty years," said Grandma. "It's never hurt me any. The trouble with all of you is—you want things too easy. You are afraid of hard work."

"Times have changed, Grandma," said Aunt Minietta.

Kayla did not like cranberry talk. She liked to eat raw cranberries right off the vine. She liked the sauce Mother made out of them. She liked nothing better than a day in the cranberry bog.

Every year since she was a baby, she had gone with Mother to the bog. First she had slept in a basket. Then she had learned to walk in the bog. When she grew older, she ran in the bog and fell in the ditches. She could not remember how many times she had fallen in! Mother always took extra clothes along. She would change each time she got wet.

Now she was tired of cranberry talk. She picked up a blanket and walked off with it.

"Come with me, Aunt Pell," she said.

Next to Grandma, Kayla loved Aunt Pell. She did not seem like an aunt. She was not cross like Aunt Tana, or hard like Aunt Donna, or fussy like Aunt Minietta. She was just a good friend.

After they rested a while, Kayla told Aunt Pell about Grandma's jewelry. She told her about wearing the pretty gold pin. Then she showed her the little fishes in the gallon bottle.

Aunt Pell always understood.

Mother May I?

Mother, may I
    go to the bog?
Yes, if you will
    sit on a log.

Mother, may I
    use a scoop?
Yes, if you will
    loop the loop.

Mother, may I
    catch a fish?
Yes, if you don't
    fall in the ditch.

Mother, may I
    eat a cake?
No, you'll get the
    tummy ache!

CHAPTER THREE

Kayla's Secret

"Today, can I go?" asked Kayla.

It was early one Saturday morning in September. Cranberry picking had started the week before.

"There is no school today," said Mother. "Yes, you can go."

Kayla jumped up and down. She was very happy.

"It is cold this morning," she said. "I will need *three* coats!"

Grandma brought out her cranberry scoop. It was like a square flat box, open at one end. On the bottom, eighteen inches long, pointed wooden teeth jutted out. It had two handles across the top.

Grandma's scoop was old and worn. She had used it for many years. The teeth had sharp points. She rubbed them with soap to make them smooth.

She smiled at Kayla. "When I stick it in the vines," she said, "the berries come up easy."

"Don't stand there, Kayla," said Mother. "Go and get ready. Put on your boots—the vines will be wet."

Kayla went in the bedroom. She closed the door behind her.

Mother packed the lunch in the kitchen. She put food in paper bags. Grandma put a pot of *munchoop* in a basket, with a dishtowel on top. *Munchoop* was something like succotash. It was made of meat and corn and lima beans and cabbage. It was a favorite dish of the Portuguese people.

Father and the boys had already gone to the store at the corner.

Mother and Grandma wore loose shirts and slacks. They put on sweaters and coats. They tied scarves round their heads. They put straw hats on top. They picked up their scoops. They waited by the door.

"Come, Kayla!" called Mother.

But Kayla did not come.

"What is she doing?" asked Grandma. "Why is she so slow?"

"Kayla! Kayla!" called Mother. "The truck is waiting for us down at the store."

Still Kayla did not come.

"Come now or we will go without you, Kayla," said Mother.

At last the bedroom door opened. Kayla came out wearing blue jeans. Her face was very red. She had her blue sweater on. It was buttoned up tight to the neck. She looked very sober. She did not look happy at all.

"What is the matter?" asked Grandma.

"What were you doing?" asked Mother. "Where are your coats? Where is your scarf? You stay an hour in there, and still you are not ready. I thought you wanted to go so bad."

"I do, but . . ." began Kayla.

"Go get your two coats," said Mother. "Bring an extra pair of blue jeans because . . ."

"You might fall in the ditch!" added Grandma, laughing.

But Kayla did not laugh. She brought the coats and put them on. She tied on the scarf.

She walked behind her mother and grandmother. At the end of Aunt Tana's Lane, they
turned the corner. They came to the store of
Peter Dias.

Every year the Santos family picked for Mr.
Jim Hubbard. He had many bogs. He sent
trucks to take his pickers to the bog. Sometimes
they picked in one bog, sometimes in another.
They went wherever the truck took them.

The first truck had already gone. Father and the boys were on it, with other people.

Mother went in the store of Peter Dias. She bought soda to drink and a seven-cent cake for each one in the family. Grandma and Kayla waited outside. It was cold. A chilly breeze blew in from the sea. The sun was not very high. It was still early in the morning.

Kayla kept her mouth shut tight. She did

not talk. She looked as if she were keeping a secret.

Grandma looked hard at her.

"You don't want to go, little chicken?" she asked.

"Oh yes," said Kayla. "Yes. I want to go."

"You don't look happy, little birdie," said Grandma. "Tell Grandma what is the matter."

Kayla shook her head. "Nothing is the matter. I'm all right."

Aunt Minietta and Aunt Tana came up with Ruby and Nancy. Aunt Donna brought Marcella and Bubba. Mrs. Lopez came with her girls and Mrs. Mendes with Sistie. Grandma spoke to them.

The driver, whose name was Burt, put a short ladder at the back of the truck. Inside were three benches. The top was covered with canvas.

They all climbed the ladder. They sat down

on the benches. Burt waited, but no one else came. So he started off.

The truck moved down the highway. It turned a corner and went down a country road. There were bogs on both sides. In some of them, people were picking.

The women laughed and talked. The girls began to sing. First they sang school songs. Then they sang a Portuguese song. It was about a soldier and the girl he loved.

Grandma smiled when she heard it. It made her think of the old country.

Only Kayla did not open her mouth.

"What's bitin' you, Kayla—a mosquito?" asked Aunt Tana. "Did you get out of bed on the wrong side this morning?"

Kayla hung her head. She did not answer.

Izzie Lopez began to tease her. "Kayla's got a secret! Kayla's got a secret and she won't tell!"

"I bet I can make her laugh," said Sistie Mendes.

Sistie leaned over and whispered to Kayla.

Kayla burst out laughing. They all laughed with her. The truck bounced over a rut. They all screamed. Little Bubba began to cry. Aunt Donna gave him a banana.

Now the truck turned into the bog. It followed a road on top of a dike, called "the

shore." The cranberries were planted on level land lower down. Ditches filled with water crossed the bog fifty feet apart.

The truck stopped and everybody got out.

Another truck bringing empty boxes, came up. The driver unloaded them. The boys from the first truck came to help. They threw the boxes across the ditch in a huge pile.

The people began to jump over the ditch.

Mr. Jim Hubbard, the owner of the bog, came up. He was stout, and had sharp blue eyes. He wore a brown lumber jacket and a small cap.

"Wait a minute," he called.

He brought a heavy plank. He laid it across the ditch. It sloped down to the bog level.

The children ran down the plank. Some pushed boxes down. Some climbed in boxes and slid down. The plank was fun.

Kayla was happy now. She waved her hands and danced down the plank. She forgot her trouble. She was happy to be in the cranberry bog. The bog was beautiful—a rich dark red from the crop of ripe berries.

Burt, the driver, took the benches out of the truck. He set them on shore. The women put their bags of lunch in the shade of the benches. Aunt Tana had a red crayon. She wrote *Tana* on her bag. She looked at the Lopez girls.

"See my name on there?" she said. "That's so they don't get mixed up."

Mother said, "Here Kayla, take the soda and put it in the ditch to keep cool."

Lukie Lima came up. "I'll do it for you, Kayla," he said.

He carried the soda bottles down the plank. Kayla followed him. He took string from his pocket. He tied it to the bottles. Then he tied the strings to a stick. He let the bottles down into the ditch. The water was deep and it was cold.

A frog jumped out of the way.

"Catch it!" cried Kayla.

But the frog was gone.

"Too late," said Lukie.

"Kayla! Kayla!" called Mother.

Kayla ran back to her mother.

"You must help, Kayla. You must give boxes to Aunt Tana."

Burt, the driver, brought scoops from the shed. He passsd them out to those who did not have their own.

Tex, the tally keeper, came up with his chart and pencil. He wrote the names of all the pickers on his chart.

"Start picking, everybody!" he called out.

The people did not wait to be told. They were already on their knees in a row. Julio took a scoop, too.

"Boxes! Boxes!" they cried.

The children ran and picked up empty boxes. Cousin Don took boxes to Father, and Roberto to Mother. Kayla put a box on her head. She took two more, one in each hand. She went to find Aunt Tana.

Aunt Tana was talking to Mrs. Lopez.

"Please may I have my scoop, Della?" asked Aunt Tana, politely.

"*Your* scoop?" said Mrs. Lopez. "This is *my*

scoop! I picked with it all last year."

"It's mine!" cried Aunt Tana. "I marked it
with red crayon on the handle. I wrote funny
things on it, so if somebody tries to take it . . ."

"I don't believe you," said Mrs. Lopez.

"What's the trouble here?" Jim Hubbard,
the bog owner, came up quietly.

"She's got my scoop," said Aunt Tana. "I
can't pick with no other scoop."

Jim Hubbard called to Burt. He came up

with three scoops. He held them out.

"Take your pick," said Jim Hubbard. "These are all good ones."

Aunt Tana took a scoop from Burt.

The two men walked off.

Aunt Tana looked angrily at Della Lopez. Della was already on her knees, scooping fast. Her two girls were giving her boxes.

"Well," said Aunt Tana in a loud voice, "if you're gonna make such a fuss over it, keep it. Maybe I'll make more anyway."

Aunt Tana was a faster picker than Mrs. Lopez. Kayla was sure of that.

Aunt Tana rocked her scoop up and down in the low-growing vines. The long teeth pulled the cranberries off. The scoop gathered up a half bushel of berries in one bite. Aunt Tana scooped to the left, then to the right, then straight ahead. She dumped the berries into the box behind her. Two scoops filled the box.

The berries looked pretty and red in the box. Kayla picked some up and ate them. She liked the taste.

Aunt Tana picked fast. Each time she filled a box, she called out, *"Fifteen!"* With her red crayon, she put an X on the box.

Aunt Tana's number was *fifteen*. When she called it, Tex came running. He put a mark by her number on his chart.

The picking was "piece work." The people were paid so much a box. This is why they picked so fast.

The long line of pickers moved quickly across the bog. The slower ones were left behind. Aunt Tana and Della Lopez were soon far ahead.

Kayla watched. It was an exciting race.

She had to run quickly back and forth, to keep Aunt Tana in boxes. Little frogs kept hopping out of the vines in front of Aunt Tana.

Kayla watched them, laughing.

The sun came up over the pine trees. It dried the dew on the cranberry vines. It shone hot and bright.

Kayla felt too warm. She took off her top coat. She kept on running, and again she felt too warm. She took off her next coat. Now she still had her sweater on, buttoned up to the neck.

The girls called her and she ran over to the ditch.

They had all been running. It was hot in the bog now. They had shed their coats and scarves. They took off their sweaters and tied them around their waists.

Only Kayla still wore hers, buttoned up tight to her neck.

"Ain't you hot?" asked Josie. "Why don't you take your sweater off?"

Kayla tossed her head.

"That's a secret," she said.

A whisper went round the group. They all looked at Kayla.

Kayla held up her chin and said:

> *"I've got a secret*
> *And I won't tell!*
> *Two green apples*
> *Dropped down a well.*
>
> *One was red*
> *And one was blue;*
> *Now you tell me*
> *What should I do?"*

CHAPTER FOUR

Kayla's Loss

"It looks easy," said Kayla. "I know I can do it."

Kayla saw an unused scoop not far away. She picked it up and dropped on her knees.

Sistie's mother and Mrs. Dias were scooping near by. They were working slowly but steadily.

"I'm going to rest all winter after I get through," said Mrs. Dias.

"It's going to be a hard winter, they say," said Mrs. Mendes.

She turned to Kayla. "That's not the right way, Kayla," she said. "Press down on the back with your left hand. Lift the front handle with your right. Let the round part rock on the ground. That makes the teeth go into the *top* of the vines. The berries are on top, not down at the roots."

Kayla tried again. This time she got some berries in her scoop. She dumped them in a box. She looked at her scoop and saw that one tooth was broken.

She dropped it quickly. She ran back to her mother.

"Oh, Mother!" she cried. "I broke a tooth!"

"Let's see," said Mother. "Open your mouth."

"Oh, not in my mouth—on my scoop!" cried Kayla.

They all laughed.

"Put that broken scoop up on shore," said Mother.

"A new one costs twenty-eight dollars," said Mrs. Dias. "They used to cost only fourteen."

Far ahead, Aunt Tana was calling out, "Boxes! Boxes!" But Kayla did not go. Aunt Tana had to call Cousin Don to help her.

Way over at the far side of the bog, Kayla saw Grandma picking. Mr. Hubbard gave her a patch all to herself. Grandma carried full boxes of cranberries on her head. She was very strong. She took them over to the wheelbarrow.

Jake, the "wheeler," loaded them on. He wheeled them across the bog and up the plank. Another man loaded them on the truck, to take them to the screen house.

Back by the ditch, another truckload of boxes

had been dumped. The children were playing
with them.

Cousin Nancy and Timmy Lima made a
house out of the boxes. They went inside with
Sistie Mendes. Lukie and Roberto and Joey
Mendes climbed on top. Kayla crawled in the
door. The boys began to pound on the roof.

"Stop that!" cried Kayla.

Suddenly the house fell to pieces. Boxes came
down on the girls' heads. Timmy began to cry.
The girls jumped up and laughed.

Off in the bog, Father called Roberto. He
was thirsty. He told Roberto to get drinking
water. The boys ran to the truck.

As soon as the boys left, the girls crowded
close around Kayla.

"Tell us your secret," they begged.

Kayla unbuttoned her sweater. She whispered her secret. Then she buttoned her
sweater up again.

"I seen better ones in the dime store," said Izzie Lopez.

"No, you never," said Sistie Mendes. "Not like this."

"Did Grandma say you could take it?" asked cousin Nancy.

"Don't let your Mother see it!" warned Josie.

Kayla made the girls promise they would not tell.

At noon, all the pickers were tired. They

were glad to stop. They came on shore to eat lunch.

Kayla and the girls ran over to join them.

It was like a picnic. Men, women and children sat on boxes, benches or upturned scoops. Some ate Portuguese food. Some ate American sandwiches.

Kayla ran to get the bottles of soda from the ditch. She leaned over to pull up the strings. She leaned too far, and down she went—splash! into the water.

"Help! Help!" she cried.

The girls came running. Josie and Sistie pulled her out.

"Oh, I've got a frog in my boot!" cried Kayla.

The girls laughed. They thought she was joking.

"The little fishes are biting me!"

Kayla shook the water off. She was wet to

her waist. She sat down on the ground. Sistie helped her pull off her boot. A tadpole fell out.

"See! I told you so!" cried Kayla.

"Good thing it wasn't a bullfrog!" laughed Josie.

"What will your mother say, when she sees you all wet?" asked Sistie.

Kayla looked worried. "Maybe she won't see it," she said.

She picked up the bottles of soda. The girls went to the shore where the people were eating.

A quarrel had started. Aunt Tana was shouting.

"I told her it was *my* scoop!" she cried.

Mrs. Lopez had left her scoop for a minute while she talked to Tex, the tally keeper. Aunt Tana, watching her chance, had picked it up.

"Look, everybody!" cried Aunt Tana. "It *is* my scoop. I picked with it all last summer. Look here! I marked it. I wrote funny things

on it. Here it says: *Funny Face* and *Fatso.*
Here it says: *Bright Eyes!*"

The children crowded round to see. Kayla
was glad Aunt Tana had found her own scoop.

"It's yours, all right," said Tex. "I remember you wrote things on it last year."

Mrs. Lopez walked away. She asked Burt
for another scoop. She did not look at the
crowd. She went back to the bog. She began
picking again.

The quarrel was settled now.

Kayla went over to Mother. Mother passed
out sandwiches. Grandma took the kettle of
munchoop out of the basket. Father and the
boys were eating. Kayla set the soda bottles
down.

Mother stared at Kayla.

"Look at that girl!" cried Mother. "All wet
to her waist!"

"She falls in the ditch the first day she comes

to the bog," said Grandma, laughing.

Roberto began to tease her:

> *"Kayla's a witch,*
> *She fell in the ditch!*
> *Who pulled her out?*
> *Little Johnny Kraut!"*

"Don't say that! Don't say that!" Kayla stamped her foot.

"Could you not see the plank?" asked Father sternly.

"I brought extra blue jeans," said Mother. "Go to the truck, Kayla, and put them on! Put the wet ones on the grass to dry."

Soon Kayla came back, eager to eat.

"Silly girl!" said Mother. "It's *hot*, don't you know it? Why don't you take your sweater off?"

Kayla picked up a sandwich. She stuffed her mouth full. She took a bottle of soda. She drank to wash the food down.

Already the men and women were going back to work. They did not want to waste a minute.

At the back end of the truck, a group of girls were playing. Kayla went over. Izzie and Ruby climbed up the sides of the truck. They swung back and forth. Josie held to the roof and skinned the cat. Marcella and Kayla crawled up on top. They sat on the canvas and swung their legs.

The wheeler, Jake, came up. His wheelbarrow held six heavy boxes of cranberries. Three boxes made a barrel.

Jake was cross. He made the girls get down.

"You trying to bust up the truck?" he asked. "Better you stay home Saturdays. You no good for work. You only make trouble when you come to the bog."

Kayla and the girls ran away.

Over at the west side of the bog, there was a huge pile of sand. Julio and Lukie and Nicky were playing on it.

"They're playing *King on the Mountain!*" cried Izzy Lopez, pointing.

"Let's go over there," said Kayla.

The girls ran. They jumped ditches and came to the sand pile.

On top of the pile, Julio stood, shouting:

> *"King of the Mountain,*
> *Here I stand!*
> *King of the ocean*
> *And king of the land!*
>
> *King of the bog*
> *Let me be!*
> *King of the ocean*
> *And king of the sea!"*

Lukie Lima dashed up the pile. He pushed Julio off and shouted *King of the Mountain* again.

The boys and girls kept pushing each other off. They fell or jumped to the bottom. They tumbled about in the sand. They played like puppy-dogs.

Then the boys got tired and ran away. The girls went too.

The sun was getting low. It threw purple shadows over the bog. Soon it would be time to go home. The girls walked back to the truck, arm in arm. They sat down and waited.

They wished the workers would quit. Now they were all over on the far side of the field. The truck had been moved several times to keep near them.

Kayla got up. She walked down the shore path to the water can. She took a drink of water.

Lukie Lima came over. Kayla looked at him in surprise. He was wearing a cranberry necklace, two cranberry bracelets and a cranberry belt. Kayla laughed.

"I used the stems to string them," said Lukie.

"Are you a girl or a boy?" asked Kayla.

"A boy," said Lukie. "These are for my girl-friend."

"Your girl-friend? Josie Lopez?" asked Kayla.

"No–for you," said Lukie.

Kayla hung her head. Lukie took the strings of cranberries off. Kayla started to put them on.

She wanted to thank Lukie, but she was too shy. Suddenly she had an idea.

"Do you want to see something?" she asked. "Something nice? Do you want to know my secret?"

Lukie nodded. "What is it?"

"Cranberry beads are pretty," said Kayla. "But I've got something prettier."

"Show it to me," said Lukie.

Kayla unbuttoned her sweater. She looked

down on the front of her dress. The string of cranberries dropped from her hand.

"Oh, it's GONE!" she cried out. "GONE! *Oh, what will I do?*" She began to cry.

"What's gone?" asked Lukie. "Tell me."

Kayla's face was white. She could hardly speak.

"Grandma's gold pin!" she said.

Cranberry Red

A cranberry red
Fell on my head—
Oh ho! I said.

A little frog
Sat on a log
In a cranberry bog.

A turtle slow
Just doesn't know
Where to go.

Sometimes I eat
A cranberry sweet
Just for a treat.

I play the witch,
I jump the ditch
And in I pitch!

CHAPTER FIVE

Kayla's Search

"But I've *got* to go, Mother!" said Kayla.

Saturday had come again, and it was time to go to the bog.

All week long, Kayla had acted sick. Mother thought she was taking the flu. But she did not seem to have a cold.

Kayla's secret lay heavy on her heart. She

hated the bog now, because trouble came to her there. But she had to go.

Mother wanted her to stay with Aunt Pell. But Grandma said, "Let her come with us."

When they reached the bog, Kayla followed Grandma. The old lady wasted no time. She set to work and soon filled a box with cranberries. She carried it on her head to the wheelbarrow.

"You want me to give you boxes?" asked Kayla.

"No, little chickie," said Grandma. "I get them myself. You go play with the girls. You go have a good time."

Kayla walked slowly back, keeping her eyes on the ground. She kept hoping she might find a glint of gold in the cranberry vines.

"Kayla! Kayla!" Aunt Tana called sharply.

Kayla hurried over. Aunt Tana was picking beside Mrs. Lopez again.

"Don't be so lazy, Kayla!" said Aunt Tana. "Bring boxes! Boxes!"

Kayla ran back to get them. She stopped beside Mother.

"Look at Tana and Della, racing again," said Mother.

Aunt Donna laughed.

"That Tana!" she cried. "She can't even tie her shoestring if the crop is good! She goes like a streak of lightning!"

"If she keeps on going so fast," said Mother, "she'll land in the ditch some day!"

Kayla brought three boxes to Aunt Tana. She went back to the pile to get more.

"Where's my box?" cried Aunt Tana. She turned to Mrs. Lopez. "You dumped in my box, Della Lopez!"

"I did *not,*" said Mrs. Lopez. "My boxes are over here. You think I want to help *you?*"

"You stole that box off me," said Aunt Tana.

"I had it half full. There's my red X on it."

"If I did," said Della Lopez, "I'll give you a full scoop."

She dumped a scoopful into Tana's box.

"A scoopful of *vines* you give me, not berries!" Tana dumped them out angrily.

Tana took her red crayon from her pocket. She marked the boxes Kayla brought her with large red X's. Mrs. Lopez paid no attention.

She looked the other way. Aunt Tana put her coat in one box, her gloves in another.

"I'm a steady picker," said Della Lopez, as if to herself. "I have no time for quarrels. I have to feed my family."

Mrs. Lopez was getting ahead. Kayla wished Aunt Tana would not quarrel so much.

Over by the shore, the girls were jumping the ditch. Kayla watched them. She had tried to play with them. But they ran off without her. She had nothing to brag about today. Her secret–her secret was spoiled.

"Hurry up, Kayla!" scolded Aunt Tana. "I can fill boxes faster than you bring them. You are as slow as a turtle."

This made Kayla slower than ever. She brought three more boxes. She did not hurry. She walked as slow as a turtle.

"I'll play like I *am* a turtle!" said Kayla to herself.

"You're lazy, that's what!" cried Aunt Tana. "Do you want Della Lopez to beat me?"

"*I don't care!*" said Kayla. "*I hope she does!*"

Kayla turned on her heel and ran. Cousin Nancy or Cousin Ruby could give boxes to Aunt Tana. Kayla did not like to be scolded all the time.

She saw Nicky Lopez and Lukie Lima going off to the ditch on the far side. She followed them.

Lukie broke off two sticks from a bush in the woods. He used his knife and made sharp points on the ends.

The boys were hunting snakes and frogs. When they saw a snake, they threw their sticks at it. They tried to spear it. Soon Nicky had a dead snake hanging from his stick. And Lukie had a dead frog.

They passed by Kayla's grandmother.

"Killing snake and frog is bad," said

Grandma. "That makes it rain for two days. When it rains, we can't pick cranberries."

The boys hung their heads ashamed.

They crossed the dike and went into the next bog. This was the one that was picked the Saturday before. Kayla followed.

She would look all over the bog. She would look hard. Maybe she could find Grandma's gold pin. She tried to remember all the places where she had played.

The boys disappeared and Kayla was left alone. She walked back and forth over the bog.

The vines looked green now, not red. All the berries had been picked. The vines were trampled down, where the people had walked on them.

A small gold pin! With pearls in it, too! How could she ever see it? It was gone, gone forever.

Kayla looked and looked. Suddenly she saw something shiny. She picked it up. It was only a piece of glass from a broken soda bottle. She kept on looking.

Once she heard a tiny noise. *Squeak, squeak, squeak!* What was it? She looked all around. There was a little nest of field mice right in the bog! The baby mice were soft and silky. She wanted to pick them up. But she was afraid to. They might bite her.

She walked on, still looking. After a while,

she found a bird's nest. Three baby birds were in it. They opened their mouths wide. She broke a cranberry in pieces. She fed them bits of cranberry.

She walked on, her eyes on the ground, looking and looking. If only she could find Grandma's gold pin. She would put it back in the olive-wood box. She would never unlock Grandma's trunk and take it out again. She would promise never to touch it again. If only she could find the gold pin!

Suddenly she heard a loud buzzing. Bees were flying around her head. What if she got stung? Timmy Lima walked into a hornet's nest once. His mother put wet mud on the sting right away. But it swelled up just the same. She ran fast to get away from the swarm of bees.

A bird flew past Kayla's head. It swooped so low, it almost struck her. She ducked as it passed. She cried out in alarm.

"Don't be afraid," said a man's voice. "The bird won't hurt you."

There was Mr. Hubbard, the bog owner. He was walking in the bog, too.

"That was a swallow," said Mr. Hubbard. "It flew into the birdhouse over there."

There were many bird boxes on posts in the ditches. Birds were flying in and out—starlings and martins and swallows and bluebirds.

"The bees and the birds are our friends here," said Mr. Hubbard.

Mr. Hubbard would not let the boys kill the birds or even shoot at them. Kayla knew that. Her brothers knew it, too.

"The bees fertilize the blossoms. The birds eat the insects," Mr. Hubbard said.

Mr. Hubbard had hives of bees in some of his bogs. He had put up all the birdhouses. He wanted the birds to come.

"Sometimes flocks of gulls come flying over from the ocean," he said. "They fly to a sand dune back of the next bog."

The man and the little girl walked on. They came to a marshy place, where high grass grew in water. A wild duck flew up from the grass.

"The ducks build their nests in this pond," said Mr. Hubbard. "The young ones are learning to fly. Before winter comes, they will all fly south. They go where it's warm in winter."

"I've seen them," said Kayla. "Every evening a flock of wild ducks used to fly over our
house. They said *honk, honk, honk!*"

"I'm putting up boxes for the wood ducks,"
said Mr. Hubbard, "over by the reservoir. The
wild birds are our friends, too."

"I like the birds," said Kayla. She told Mr.
Hubbard about the nest on the ground. She
told him about the field mice.

"But what are you doing here alone?" asked
Mr. Hubbard.

"I'm looking for something," said Kayla.
"Something I lost last Saturday."

"It's pretty hard to find things in the cranberry vines," said Mr. Hubbard. "What was
it?"

Kayla's face fell. All her old worry came
back. Should she tell her secret?

"Maybe I can find it for you," said Mr.
Hubbard.

Kayla thought deeply. Then she spoke.

"It's this way, Mr. Hubbard," she said. "This is your bog. So I think you ought to know there's a gold pin in it. A beautiful gold brooch with pearls."

Mr. Hubbard said, "Oh?"

Then he asked, "Whose gold pin?"

"My grandma's," said Kayla.

"Did she lose it?"

"No," said Kayla. "*I* did."

Mr. Hubbard did not act surprised or angry.

Kayla went on with a rush of words. "I took it without telling Grandma and then I lost it, but she don't know it's lost, because I'm going to find it—I'm sure I will find it. I'm going to put it back before she even knows it's gone!"

"I wish I could help you," said Mr. Hubbard. "But it's very hard to find things lost in a bog."

"Is it?" asked Kayla. Her heart sank.

"Yes," said Mr. Hubbard. "Now let us go to your Mother. I am sure she is looking for you."

They walked on. Kayla shivered. A cold wind was blowing. She wished she had her coat.

"It's going to frost tonight," said Mr. Hubbard. "I heard it on the radio. We'll have to flood the bogs to save the berries."

"Flood the bogs?" cried Kayla. "With water?"

They crossed the dike and walked toward the truck.

Lukie Lima came running up. He had a small turtle in one hand. He said he found it in the ditch.

"What are you going to do with it?" asked Mr. Hubbard.

"Give it to Kayla," said Lukie. "She likes pets."

Kayla took the turtle. She handled it gingerly. She liked little fishes and baby mice and baby birds. But she was not sure she liked frogs and turtles.

"The turtle is getting dry from the wind," said Mr. Hubbard. "He's been out of water too long. He doesn't like that."

Lukie and Kayla looked at the turtle.

"Do you know how to take care of it, Kayla?" asked Mr. Hubbard.

"No," said Kayla.

"Take him home and put him in a pan of water with a few stones," said Mr. Hubbard. "Change the water every day and feed him."

Mother was standing beside the truck. She saw the turtle in Kayla's hand.

"What's that you got, Kayla?" she asked.

"A turtle," said Kayla. "Buy him some turtle food, Mother."

"I don't know how to feed a turtle," said Mother.

Mr. Hubbard spoke up. "Give him crumbs and hamburger, Mrs. Santos. A little will last a long time."

Kayla climbed up in the truck. Soon she was on her way home.

But Grandma's gold pin was still lost in the bog.

CHAPTER SIX

Kayla's Confession

"You must wear your coat to school," said Mother.

"It's too heavy," said Kayla. "It's not winter yet."

"The radio says it will be cold all week," said Mother. "I hope the cranberries don't get frozen. In one more week, we will be done picking."

Father had been up all night. The bogs had to be flooded to save the crop. Each bog had its own pump house to pump water from the reservoir. Father worked all night with the men. They opened the sluices and ran water into the ditches. The water ran over the bog itself. It covered the vines two or three inches deep.

At four in the morning, the water was drained off. With a good breeze and a bright sun, the vines dried quickly. The people picked again next day. Soon all Mr. Hubbard's bogs would be picked. His crop would be saved.

Kayla went to the bog on the last day. It was a Saturday in early November. She had not been to the bog since the day she told Mr. Hubbard about the lost pin.

She hated to go. She did not want to think about the gold pin. She tried to tell herself that Grandma never even missed it!

But today was the Bog Party! She had to be there for that! All the girls would be there. It was the most fun of all.

The old people picked cranberries until noon. The boys and girls played with the empty boxes. They used them for boats in the ditches. They made tents and forts. They beat on them with sticks for drums. They jumped the ditches and fell in. They caught frogs and turtles.

Kayla was happy again. She loved the bog as much as ever.

At noon, the picking was done. The people all made their way to the screen house to celebrate. The men brought tables out and the women covered them with crepe paper.

Kayla and the girls helped set the table. Baskets and baskets of food had been brought from home.

Mother and Grandma had made *Kanjshá* in their biggest pot. This was chicken fricassee,

Portuguese style, highly seasoned. There were other good things too—potato salad, potato chips, pickled pigs' feet, cold cuts and pickles, apple and squash pies. There was plenty of soda to drink.

Everybody crowded round the table and ate. They laughed and talked and made jokes. Old and young had fun together.

Then the dancing began.

The women looked pretty, dressed in gay costumes. They wore necklaces and bracelets of cranberries. Aunt Tana and Della Lopez forgot their quarrels and were friends again.

The men brought guitars and played. Peter Dias brought a record-player with Spanish and Portuguese records. When he turned them on, the old ladies took the old men by the arms and danced round the bog. They made a big circle.

They danced till they were tired.

Then they sang and played. They laughed and told jokes. Everybody was happy. The crop was a good one. They had worked hard. Mr. Hubbard had paid everybody off. They had earned enough to carry them through the coming year.

Kayla and the other children danced and played. They threw cranberries at each other.

At last they all went home. Cranberry picking was over for another year.

In the week that followed, Mother and Father went to the store to buy winter food supplies. They bought one-hundred-pound bags of sugar, rice and dried lima beans. They bought large bags of potatoes. They bought a case of canned milk and a case of canned peas. They bought everything wholesale.

When all the things were unloaded at the house on Aunt Tana's Lane, Grandma said,

"God has been good to us. We will eat well this winter. We must not forget to thank Him."

Soon would come a special feast day at church. A pole would be set up like the mast of a ship. From it would hang streamers, decorated with strings of cranberries and other fruits. A procession would march around with a man beating a drum. After prayers and a dance, the fruit would be distributed.

Everybody got ready to go to the Feast. Grandma put on her best dress, her black silk which she wore only for special occasions.

"Come, Kayla," said Grandma. "You must dress quickly, so you will not be late."

Kayla started to get ready. She washed carefully. She combed and brushed her hair. Mother braided it and tied the ribbons on. Kayla went in the bedroom to get her Sunday dress.

Grandma was on her knees beside the bed. She had the trunk key in her hand. She unlocked the trunk.

Kayla watched, her heart beating fast.

"Maybe she's just getting out her silk shawl," said Kayla to herself.

But Grandma did not touch the shawl. She picked up the olive-wood box.

Kayla did not move. She trembled where she stood. She could not keep her eyes off the olive-wood box.

Grandma opened it. She picked up her gold bracelet and put it on. She put her gold earrings in her ears. Then she looked again. She was looking for something else.

"Where is my gold pin?" asked Grandma.

Her voice was tight and hard. "I will wear my gold pin today—on this special Feast Day."

Kayla turned and slipped out of the room. She rushed through the kitchen. She ran outside, just as she was. She crossed the yard to the hen house. She went inside and closed the door behind her.

Grandma had found her out at last.

Her heart was pounding hard. She covered her face and began to cry. The hens, frightened, ran out into the chicken yard. Kayla was left alone.

She waited a long time.

"Kayla! Kayla!" called Mother from the back door. "Come, Kayla! It is time to go to church."

Kayla did not answer.

"Kayla! Kayla!" called Grandma from the front door. Again Kayla did not answer.

She listened carefully.

"Where has she gone?" she heard Mother say. Mother was out in the yard now. "She wore only her slip. She had no dress on. She couldn't go far like that."

Kayla heard the boys running and calling her in loud voices. No one thought of looking in the hen house. There Kayla was safe.

At last, Kayla heard a car drive up. Kayla peeped out the tiny window. She saw Mother and Grandma, Father and the boys getting into Uncle Diamond's car. They were going to church. They were going without her.

She opened the door, came outside and went back in the house. It was quiet and empty with no one there. A pot of delicious food simmered on the oil stove. She sniffed it hungrily.

She went in the bedroom.

Grandma's trunk was closed and locked again. It was under the bed in its usual place.

Kayla put on her best dress. Then she walked down Aunt Tana's Lane. She knew she should have gone to church, but she was afraid to see her family, afraid to face Grandma.

She passed Aunt Pell's house. In the yard, she saw Aunt Pell. She went in to talk to her. Aunt Pell had been to church early. She sat on the couch to talk to Kayla.

Kayla leaned on her shoulder. Next to

Grandma, Kayla loved Aunt Pell. Aunt Pell always understood her. Maybe Aunt Pell could help.

The next minute Kayla burst into tears. It wasn't long before the whole story came out.

Aunt Pell did not act surprised or angry. She thought a while. Then she spoke gently.

"You will have to tell them, Kayla," said Aunt Pell. "Once you tell it, it will be a load off your heart. Then your conscience will be clear."

"But they will punish me," said Kayla.

"Don't you think you should be punished?" asked Aunt Pell gently.

Slowly, Kayla nodded. "I guess so," she said.

When the family came home from church, they found Aunt Pell there with Kayla. Aunt Pell went in the bedroom with Grandma and they talked together. Aunt Pell called Kayla,

and she went in, too. When she came out later, her eyes were very red.

Aunt Pell told the family that Grandma's gold pin was lost in the bog.

Kayla said she was sorry she took it and wore it. Kayla sat in the big arm chair. Everybody stared at her. They were surprised that she had done such a thing.

Kayla tried to explain. "It was so pretty . . ."

she said. "I just wanted to wear it once . . ."

"Once!" cried Aunt Tana. "Once–to the cranberry bog!"

Aunt Tana and Uncle Diamond and Nancy had come in. Aunt Tana spoke to Mother. "She ought to be punished severely."

Mother did not answer.

Father said, "We will go to the bog and hunt for it. We will take the whole family and everybody look. Do you remember which bog it was?"

"Oh yes!" said Kayla. How could she ever forget?

"What is the use?" said Mother. "It is too late. The bogs have been flooded. The gold pin has been washed away."

"Not that bog," said Kayla. "It was picked before frost."

"We must tell Mr. Hubbard," said Uncle Diamond. "When they screen the drops from the bog water, they might find it."

"I have told Mr. Hubbard already," said Kayla.

They looked at her in surprise.

"I told him right away," said Kayla. "He said he would help me find it. But—I guess he didn't look hard enough."

Grandma sat still on the sofa. She did not say anything. She looked very sad. Kayla wished she could bring the gold pin back and make Grandma happy again. She remembered Grandma's story. *Her* grandma gave the gold pin to her when she was married. She had promised to give it to Kayla on her wedding day. Now she would never get it.

"We will go to the bog and look," said Father.

That afternoon, the whole family went to the bog. Everybody but Grandma. She stayed home alone. The cousins and aunts and uncles all went. They tramped back and forth, but they found nothing. They soon decided the search was useless.

The air was crispy cold now with the coming of winter. The bogs would be flooded more deeply soon. The water would cover the vines entirely. It would turn the bogs into frozen lakes.

Flocks of wild ducks passed overhead, flying south. Winter was coming. Kayla shivered. She buttoned her heavy coat tighter.

When Kayla came home, she had to tell Grandma. "We did not find it, Grandma," she said.

Grandma was not cross at all. Grandma did not scold or punish her. Kayla sat on Grandma's lap. She whispered in her ear. "I don't need a present on my wedding day," she said.

Grandma smiled and put her arms around her.

Cape Cod Song

Cape Cod girls they have no combs,
They comb their hair with codfish bones!

Cape Cod boys they have no sleds,
They slide down hill on codfish heads!

Cape Cod cats they have no tails,
They blew away in heavy gales!

Cape Cod dogs they cannot bark
They're scared outside when it gets dark!

(Traditional)

CHAPTER SEVEN

Kayla's Christmas

"This one is the prettiest," said Kayla.

She pointed to a small spruce tree. Roberto took his axe and chopped it down.

Kayla and the boys were in the woods by the beach. The ground was coated with snow. It was very cold, with a hard wind blowing. The breakers were high, topped with whitecaps. The sky was dark and it began to snow again.

Kayla stamped her feet to keep warm.

"Guess we won't go in swimming today," said Julio.

"No," said Roberto. "But skating maybe—tomorrow. All the bogs are frozen solid now."

"Hurry, let's go home," said Kayla. "I'm so cold!"

She ran on ahead through the snow. The boys followed, carrying the tree between them. They walked through the woods path, crossed the highway and came to the corner by the store of Peter Dias.

Sounds of music came from inside the store. Roberto peeped in the window.

"Uncle Diamond is in there, playing his guitar," said Roberto. "Peter Dias has his accordion and Lukie Lima's father his mandolin."

"Uncle Diamond gave me his old accordion," said Julio. "He says I'll soon be as good as he is."

"Father says he'll get me a violin," said Roberto.

The children passed Aunt Tana's house. She waved to them from her back door. At the next house, Aunt Pell called to them to come in. She gave them cookies to eat. They warmed their hands by her stove.

Then they hurried on with their Christmas tree. All the way down Aunt Tana's Lane, people were getting ready for Christmas. Some put wreathes in their windows or pine branches on the door. Sounds of music came from some of the houses. Everybody was in festive spirit.

At home, Mother and Grandma had worked hard all day. Special dishes were cooked for a real Portuguese Christmas. In the kitchen, the table was already set. The best white linen table cloth had been taken from Grandma's trunk. Candles were ready to light.

Soon everything would be ready for the evening serenade. The house looked beautiful.

Roberto and Julio set up the spruce tree in the corner of the living room. Kayla hung shiny balls and strings of popcorn on. She thought it was very pretty. Mother brought out American gifts and laid them under the tree.

Father came home and everybody dressed up in his Sunday best. Then they sat down and waited.

"I hear them coming!" cried Kayla.

She went to the front window to look out. Above the pine trees across the road, she could see the moon rising in a deep blue sky. Sounds of music came closer and closer.

The serenaders were going from house to house. Not a single Portuguese home in the village would be missed. All were celebrating Christmas, the day of Christ's birth.

"Here they come! Here they come!" cried Kayla. She danced on tiptoes, she was so happy.

Father opened the front door and called in a loud voice, "Welcome! Welcome to this house on Christmas!"

Five men stood outside. They carried musical instruments. Their leader stepped up and said, "Now we enter this house with the good will of God. Blessings be upon this house at Christmas time!"

The men came in, shaking the snow off their feet. Some boys came in, too. The men tuned up their violins and guitars. Julio brought his

accordion. They played and sang carols in Portuguese.

Then the men turned to Peter Dias. He was appointed to say the prayer. It was an old traditional prayer from the old country. He sang the prayer instead of saying it. When Grandma heard it, the tears rolled down her cheeks.

Then Father invited the guests to the table in the kitchen.

Kayla had never seen the table so beautiful. With the lighted candles, it was like a feast. There were three cakes, several pies, bowls of apples, oranges and candy. There were other special Portuguese dishes.

Father said, "Here is the gift, the Christmas gift!"

He gave Peter Dias an orange. Peter put it in the bag he carried. It was the custom for the home-owner to present a gift, no matter how small.

The men and boys crowded round the table with the family. They helped themselves to food and drink. They danced around the table with joy. Christmas was a happy time for everybody.

When the serenaders left, they said, "May you live long, to see many Christmases!"

"Thank you, thank you!" called the Santos family.

On the afternoon of Christmas Day, the children went skating. Lukie Lima's father came after them in his car. He took the Lopez children and the cousins, too. The car was very crowded. They drove to one of the bogs near the ocean, where the ice was best. The boys took wide shovels and brooms and brushed the snow off.

It was Kayla's ill-fated bog. She hated to think of the trouble that had come to her there.

Kayla had received new skates for Christmas.

She changed to the skate shoes and started to
skate. At first she felt awkward. But soon she
got used to the new skates. Soon she was skating
as fast as anybody.

The boys played hockey with sticks and a
ball. The girls played *Crack the Whip.*

Izzie Lopez was the leader. She shouted:

> *"Crack the whip and let it zip,*
> *Do not fall, roll like a ball!"*

She swung the line of five girls as hard as she

could. They went sailing over the ice, Kayla on the tail end. Faster and faster she went, at last tumbling down. The girls laughed and teased her.

Now the boys stopped playing hockey. Up on shore, they built a fire. They brought wood from the pine woods near by. They fed the fire and it burned brightly. They crowded round to warm up.

The girls came over, shivering. They took sandwiches and apples from their coat pockets and ate. Cold winds blew in from the ocean, but they scarcely noticed. Hands and toes were cold, and noses were red. But skating on the bog was fun.

When the fire died down, they ran back to the ice for one last round of skating. Boys and girls formed in one long line. Julio, the oldest and strongest boy, cracked the long whip.

"Crack the whip and let her zip!" he shouted.

Away went the children, sailing over the ice. Kayla was in the middle of the line. Suddenly her ankle turned and down she went! The line broke. Two parts of the whip sailed away and left her.

Down on the ice in a huddle she lay. A sharp pain shot through her ankle. She tried to get up, but couldn't. She unstrapped her skate. She decided to walk. She took her boot off and stared at her ankle. It had begun to swell. It felt very sore. She must have twisted it.

She started to pick up her boot, then let it fall from her hand. She stared at the ice. She saw something shiny just below the surface. She could not make out what it was.

The girls came running up.

"Why don't you get up?" asked Cousin Nancy.

"Come on—we're going home," said the Lopez girls.

Sistie Mendes and Cousin Marcella tried to help Kayla up.

"I've hurt my ankle," said Kayla. "I can't walk on it."

Sistie called the boys. Julio and Roberto came over. But Kayla did not ask them to help her.

"Look!" she cried. "Look, Julio! There's something under the ice—frozen in. What is it?"

Julio got down on his knees. He took his knife out of his pocket. He used the largest blade to dig into the ice.

"Golly!" he said. "You've found something all right!"

"Once I found a can of sardines under the ice," said Nicky Lopez. "Somebody's lunch at cranberry time! It had never been opened. When we thawed it out, we ate the sardines. They were good, too."

"What do you think it is, Julio?"

Kayla hardly dared breathe. She did not dare hope. She leaned heavily on Sistie's shoulder. She forgot about her ankle.

Julio kept on digging. All the children were excited. "What is it?" they asked.

Julio brushed the ice off and held it up.

It was Grandma's gold pin!

Kayla's eyes shone as she took it in her hand. "Oh, I knew I'd find it!"

She hugged it tight. "A Christmas present for Grandma," she said.

When she reached home, Lukie Lima's father had to carry her in the house and put her on the sofa.

"She sprained her ankle and will have to stay off it for a while," he explained.

But nobody listened to him. Nobody looked at Kayla's ankle. All they could see was Grandma's gold pin in the little girl's hand.

Kayla gave the brooch to Grandma and was happy again.